LOS ANGELES CLIPPERS

by Bernie Wilson

Published by ABDO Publishing Company, 8000 West 78th Street, Edina, Minnesota 55439. Copyright © 2012 by Abdo Consulting Group, Inc. International copyrights reserved in all countries. No part of this book may be reproduced in any form without written permission from the publisher. SportsZone™ is a trademark and logo of ABDO Publishing Company.

Printed in the United States of America,
North Mankato, Minnesota
062011
092011

 THIS BOOK CONTAINS AT LEAST 10% RECYCLED MATERIALS.

Editors: Matt Tustison, Dave McMahon
Copy Editor: Nicholas Cafarelli
Series design and cover production: Christa Schneider
Interior production: Carol Castro

Photo Credits: Mark J. Terrill/AP Images, cover, 1, 7, 41, 43 (middle), 43 (bottom), 44; Chris Carlson/AP Images, 4, 9, 11; Focus on Sport/Getty Images, 12, 20, 42 (top); Dick Raphael/NBAE/Getty Images, 14; Rusty Kennedy/AP Images, 16, 42 (middle); AP Images, 19; Lenny Ignelzi/AP Images, 23; Joel Zwink/AP Images, 25; Gary Stewart/AP Images, 26; Nick Ut/AP Images, 28, 38; Stephen Dunn/NBAE/Getty Images, 31; Jim Gund/NBAE/Getty Images, 32, 42 (bottom); Getty Images, 34, 43 (top); Chris Martinez/AP Images, 37; Rene Macura/AP Images, 47

Library of Congress Cataloging-in-Publication Data
Wilson, Bernie.
  Los Angeles Clippers / by Bernie Wilson.
     p. cm. -- (Inside the NBA)
  Includes index.
  ISBN 978-1-61783-160-7
  1. Los Angeles Clippers (Basketball team)--History--Juvenile literature. I. Title.
  GV884.52.L65W55 2011
  796.323'640979494--dc22
                                  2011014724

TABLE OF CONTENTS

CASSELL
19
Clippers
50
DENVER
7
CHAPTER 1
PLAYOFF SUCCESS

When sports fans talk about the National Basketball Association (NBA) in Los Angeles, most people automatically think about Kobe Bryant and the Lakers. In the spring of 2006, however, the Los Angeles Clippers reminded fans that there are two NBA teams in the city.

The Clippers have long been considered one of the least successful franchises in sports. But they surprisingly outlasted the Lakers, one of the most successful teams in sports, in the 2006 postseason. The sixth-seeded Clippers eliminated the third-seeded Denver Nuggets four games to one in the first round of the postseason. The Lakers, meanwhile, had a poor regular season by their standards. As a result, they were only the seventh seed in the Western Conference playoffs.

Sam Cassell, *left*, and Corey Maggette celebrate during the Clippers' 101–83 win over the Denver Nuggets in their 2006 playoff series.

The second-seeded Phoenix Suns ousted the Lakers in the first round in seven games.

This meant that the Clippers and the Suns met in the second round. By advancing to the second round of the 2006 postseason, the Clippers matched the furthest play-off push in team history. The Clippers hoped to advance even further. But the Suns prevailed in seven games.

Still, the Clippers could proudly look back at one of the best seasons in club history. The Clippers seemed to come out of nowhere in the 2005–06 campaign under coach Mike Dunleavy. Of course, success usually was not expected from the Clippers. Going into that season, the franchise had qualified for the playoffs only six times. The club began play in 1970 as the Buffalo Braves. It then moved to San Diego and played there as the Clippers from 1978 to 1984. The team then relocated to Los Angeles. Along the way, the team developed a reputation for losing.

That is what made the Clippers' 2006 playoff run such a big deal. They had become legitimate contenders. Forward Elton Brand and guard

The Clippers' Elton Brand, *right*, keeps the ball away from the Memphis Grizzlies' Shane Battier in February 2006.

Sam Cassell led the 2005–06 Clippers. Los Angeles acquired Cassell from the Minnesota Timberwolves in a trade before the season. The Clippers set the stage for their playoff run by finishing second in the Pacific Division. They had the second-best record in club history at 47–35. The Clippers finished two games ahead of the Lakers. The record was the team's best since leaving Buffalo in 1978.

The Clippers had home-court advantage for their best-of-seven first-round series against the Nuggets. They used it well by winning the first two games at the Staples Center. Denver won the third game

ELTON BRAND

Burly forward Elton Brand was the best overall player on the 2005–06 Clippers.

The 6-foot-8, 275-pound Brand spent seven seasons with the Clippers, from 2001 to 2008. He played consistently well for the team. He averaged about 20 points and 10 rebounds per game. Brand had his best season in 2005–06, when he averaged 24.7 points and 10 rebounds.

Brand excelled at Duke University and turned pro after two seasons at the North Carolina school. The Chicago Bulls selected him first overall in the 1999 NBA Draft. Brand played two seasons with the Bulls, who then traded him to the Clippers.

Brand finally made his playoff debut in the 2005–06 season. The forward left as a free agent after the 2007–08 season and signed with the Philadelphia 76ers. He is remembered by Clippers fans as one of the top players in club history.

at its home arena, the Pepsi Center. But the Clippers came back to win the fourth game in Denver and then the fifth game in Los Angeles. This clinched the team's first play-off series victory in 30 years. Fans in Los Angeles were excited because the Lakers had taken a three-games-to-one lead against the Suns in their playoff series. A Clippers-Lakers matchup in the second round seemed likely. All the games would have been played at the Staples Center. That is the gleaming downtown arena that is home to both the Clippers and the Lakers.

The Lakers, however, could not hold up their end of the bargain. They dropped three games in a row to the Suns and lost the series in seven games. That sent the Clippers to Phoenix for the first two games of the second

The Clippers' Sam Cassell goes up for a shot between the Suns' Steve Nash, *left*, and James Jones during the teams' 2006 playoff series.

round. The Suns were known for their offense, with point guard Steve Nash leading the way. The first two contests were high-scoring affairs. Phoenix won the series opener 130–123. The Clippers bounced back to surprise the Suns 122–97 in Game 2.

The series shifted to Los Angeles. The teams again traded wins. The Suns won 94–91 in Game 3. The Clippers won the next game 114–107 to tie the series. Back in Phoenix, the series turned when the Suns won Game 5 in double overtime, 125–118. Phoenix's Shawn Marion collected 36 points and 20 rebounds. Brand had 33 points and 15 rebounds, and Cassell added 32 points.

Phoenix had a three-games-to-two lead and needed one more win to take the series. Brand helped keep the Clippers alive by scoring 30 points in Game 6. Host Los Angeles won 118–106. Center Chris Kaman added 15 points and 10 rebounds for the Clippers.

The teams went back to Phoenix for a Game 7 that would determine the series winner. Playing in probably their most important game ever, the Clippers faltered. The Suns rolled to a 127–107 win. Marion (30 points, nine rebounds) and Nash (29 points, 11 assists) led Phoenix. Brand had 36 points and nine rebounds for Los Angeles. Cassell was limited to 11 points. The Clippers' exciting ride ended one victory short of reaching the conference finals for the first time.

Despite the disappointment of being eliminated, the Clippers proved that they were no longer the NBA's laughingstock. They showed that they were capable of competing with the league's best teams.

"It was a coming out party for myself and teammates," Brand said. "We're only going to get better. We've got a lot of young guys on our team that are going to improve."

The Clippers' Cuttino Mobley, *right*, and Quinton Ross react during Los Angeles's 127–107 loss to Phoenix in Game 7 of the 2006 Western Conference semifinals.

Unfortunately for Los Angeles, Brand was not correct. The team reverted to its losing ways in the years following 2006. However, with star rookie forward Blake Griffin leading the way in the 2010–11 season, the team's future appeared to be bright. Griffin's emergence gave the team hope that it could break through sometime soon. Maybe the Clippers could even surpass the 2005–06 team's accomplishments.

CHAPTER 2

BORN IN BUFFALO

Los Angeles has been the Clippers' home since 1984. But not many fans realize that the club actually began play as the Buffalo Braves. Buffalo is located in western New York, about 2,500 miles (4,023 km) from Los Angeles, California.

The Braves were one of three expansion teams joining the NBA for the 1970–71 season. The Cleveland Cavaliers and the Portland Trail Blazers were the others. At the time, the NBA was competing for attention with the rival American Basketball Association (ABA).

Buffalo's first coach was Dolph Schayes. Schayes had been a star forward for the NBA's Syracuse Nationals. In the Braves' first regular-season game ever, they defeated the visiting Cavaliers 107–92 on October 14, 1970. Like most new teams, however, the Braves

Star big man Bob McAdoo shoots for the Buffalo Braves during the 1970s. The Braves began playing in 1970 as an expansion team and would later move and become the Clippers.

Buffalo's Jim McMillian rises for a jump shot during the Braves' 1974 playoff series against the Boston Celtics. The Braves fell in six games.

struggled at first. They finished 22–60 in their opening season.

The Braves added center Elmore Smith and guard Randy Smith, both rookies, and veteran guard Walt Hazzard for their second season. But they finished 22–60 again. Former Philadelphia 76ers coach Jack Ramsay became Buffalo's coach before the team's third season.

The Braves also drafted center/forward Bob McAdoo. McAdoo averaged 18.1 points and 9.1 rebounds per game and was named NBA Rookie of the Year. Nevertheless, Buffalo finished 21–61.

By the 1973–74 season, the Braves were becoming respectable. They traded Elmore Smith to the Los Angeles Lakers for forward Jim McMillian. McMillian and McAdoo helped guide the Braves to their first winning record at 42–40 and their first playoff berth.

Buffalo also received a boost from point guard Ernie DiGregorio. He averaged a league-high 8.2 assists and became the second consecutive Brave to be chosen NBA Rookie of the Year. McAdoo had developed into the league's top scorer at 30.6 points per game. In addition, he averaged 15.1 rebounds a contest. The Braves led the NBA in scoring with 111.6 points per game. But they also gave up the most points at 111.8.

Buffalo faced the Boston Celtics in the Eastern Conference semifinals. No team in NBA history had enjoyed as much success as the Celtics. The Braves put up a good fight but lost four games to two.

BOB McADOO

Bob McAdoo was the biggest star the Buffalo Braves ever had, and he probably was the top player in club history.

The Braves selected the 6-foot-9 center/forward with the second overall pick in the 1972 NBA Draft. McAdoo had been a standout at the University of North Carolina. His impact with the Braves was immediate, as he won the NBA's Rookie of the Year Award in 1973.

McAdoo captured the NBA's scoring title, his first of three straight, in 1974 and was named the league's Most Valuable Player (MVP) in 1975. McAdoo was a true standout for Buffalo, which nevertheless traded him in December 1976 after a change in ownership.

He joined the Los Angeles Lakers and won league titles in 1982 and 1985 with them under coach Pat Riley.

McAdoo was inducted into the Basketball Hall of Fame in 2000.

Buffalo's Bob McAdoo goes up with the ball as Philadelphia's George McGinnis defends in a 1976 first-round playoff series. The Braves won two games to one.

In 1974–75, the Braves had their best season in Buffalo. The team finished 49–33. Through 2010–11, that was still the top record in club history. McAdoo again led the NBA in scoring. He averaged 34.5 points along with 14.1 rebounds. Buffalo reached the postseason again and pushed the Washington Bullets to seven games in the Eastern Conference semifinals before falling. Washington would later advance to the NBA Finals and lose to the Golden State Warriors.

The Braves continued their regular-season success

in 1975–76. Ramsay guided the team to a 46–36 record. McAdoo ranked first in the NBA in scoring for the third straight season. He averaged 31.1 points per game to go with 12.4 rebounds. This time, the Braves tasted postseason success. They won a series for the first time, beating the Philadelphia 76ers two games to one in the first round. Buffalo had to face Boston in the conference semifinals, though. The Braves lost four games to two again. The Celtics would go on to win the NBA championship that season.

Unfortunately for Braves fans, it was the beginning of the end of the good times. A change in ownership before the 1976–77 season altered the positive feelings around the team. It also eventually led to a move to California. John Y. Brown had formerly owned the ABA's Kentucky Colonels. He bought half of the Braves from Paul Snyder prior to the 1976–77 campaign and then bought the other 50 percent late in the season.

In September 1976, Buffalo sold McMillian's contract rights to the New York Knicks. Two months later, the Braves

Jack Ramsay

Jack Ramsay was the coach of all three of the Braves' playoff teams. He coached Buffalo for four seasons from 1972 to 1976. Ramsay enjoyed a long and successful career as an NBA coach and executive. He was general manager of the Philadelphia 76ers in the 1960s, helping the team win the NBA championship in 1967. He coached the 76ers from 1968 to 1972 before taking the job with the Braves. After leaving Buffalo, he took over as coach of the Portland Trail Blazers and led them to the NBA title in 1977. He has done commentary on television and he has a doctorate in education from the University of Pennsylvania. That is why he is sometimes referred to as "Dr. Jack Ramsay."

traded McAdoo and center Tom McMillen to New York for $3 million and center John Gianelli. The Braves received solid play in 1976–77 from forward Adrian Dantley. He was named NBA Rookie of the Year. But the team had lost some of its best players. The Braves went through three coaches that season and tumbled to a 30–52 record. With the drop in performance came a drop in attendance. Brown renegotiated his lease to include an escape clause. The clause would allow him to move the team out of Buffalo if attendance fell below a certain level.

Before the 1977–78 season, the Braves traded Dantley to the Indiana Pacers and acquired star guard Nate "Tiny" Archibald from the New Jersey Nets. The Braves sent two first-round draft choices to the Nets as part of the deal. Archibald injured his ankle during training camp and missed the entire season. He would never play a game for the club. The Braves sank to a 27–55 record in what was to be their final season in Buffalo.

Brown had wanted a new city for his team to call home. The Braves competed for fans in Buffalo with the popular Bills of the National Football League and the Sabres of the NHL.

NBA attorney David Stern, who later became the league's commissioner, came up with an idea. He proposed that the

Buffalo's Billy Knight looks to pass as Chicago's Scott May defends him in November 1977. In the club's last season in Buffalo, the Braves finished with a 27–55 record.

Braves move to San Diego, California, and that Brown swap franchises with Irv Levin. Levin was the owner of the Celtics. The deal included a seven-player trade in which Boston obtained Archibald, guard Billy Knight, and forward Marvin Barnes. The Celtics also kept the draft rights to forward Larry Bird. Bird would become one of the NBA's all-time greats. San Diego received guard Freeman Williams, center Kevin Kunnert, and forwards Kermit Washington and Sidney Wicks.

With that, the NBA left western New York and returned to sunny San Diego.

CHAPTER 3
SAILING IN
SAN DIEGO

San Diego had already been host to an NBA team before the Buffalo Braves moved across the country prior to the 1978–79 season.

San Diego, located in Southern California, once had an NBA franchise named the Rockets. They began playing in 1967. The Rockets had four losing seasons. Owner Bob Breitbard then sold the team to Texas businessmen, who moved the club to Houston.

The Braves received a new nickname, the Clippers, with the move to San Diego. The name referred to a kind of sailing ship, a clipper, that passed through San Diego Bay. The Clippers would play at the San Diego Sports Arena, just as the Rockets had.

With a new home and new name, the Clippers hired Gene Shue as their coach before the 1978–79 season. Shue had

The Clippers' World B. Free shoots against the Nets during the 1978–79 campaign. Before that season, the Buffalo Braves moved to San Diego and became the Clippers.

previously been coach of the Baltimore Bullets and the Philadelphia 76ers. San Diego also had acquired a new star, Lloyd B. Free. Free would later legally change his name to World B. Free. San Diego obtained Free in a trade with Philadelphia. He had been a good player with the 76ers.

But he came into his own with the Clippers. He averaged 28.8 points per game in the 1978–79 season. He had the second-best scoring average after the San Antonio Spurs' George Gervin. Free helped the Clippers finish 43–39. But that mark was not good enough to earn San Diego a postseason berth in a tough Western Conference.

Before the 1979–80 season, the Clippers made news when they acquired San Diego native Bill Walton. The 6-foot-11 center had helped the Portland Trail Blazers win the NBA title in 1977. He was named the league's MVP after the 1977–78 season. Walton had played at Helix High School in La Mesa, a suburb of San Diego. He then starred at University of California, Los Angeles (UCLA). He helped the Bruins win two National Collegiate Athletic Association (NCAA) championships.

San Diego native Bill Walton speaks to the media in May 1979 after he signed with the Clippers. Injuries would hamper him while he was with the team, though.

But Walton had a history of foot and ankle injuries. Those ailments would keep him off the court frequently during his time with the Clippers. Walton missed the entire 1980–81 and 1981–82 campaigns and big parts of his three other seasons with San Diego.

Walton played in only 14 games in his first season in San Diego in 1979–80. He watched as the Clippers sank to 35–47. The Clippers had given up a lot to get Walton: a first-round draft pick, guard Randy Smith, forward Kermit Washington, and center Kevin Kunnert.

"THE BIG REDHEAD"

Bill Walton is one of the most popular figures in San Diego sports history, even though his time with the hometown Clippers from 1979 to 1985 was marred by injuries.

Affectionately known as "the big redhead," the center won NBA titles before and after he was a Clipper. He was an NBA champion with the Portland Trail Blazers in 1977 and with the Boston Celtics in 1986. He went on to become a successful NBA broadcaster.

Walton will always be linked to the great John Wooden teams at UCLA, where he played from 1971 to 1974. He helped the Bruins to national titles in 1972 and 1973. As great as his basketball career was, Walton was equally proud that all four of his sons played college basketball. One of his sons, Luke, starred at the University of Arizona and was drafted by the Lakers. Luke won NBA titles with the Lakers in 2009 and 2010.

The trade would hurt the Clippers in future seasons.

The Clippers struggled to win games. But some of their players did enjoy personal success. Free finished second to the Spurs' Gervin in scoring for a second season in a row. Free increased his average to 30.2 points. Meanwhile, Clippers center Swen Nater won the NBA's rebounding title. He averaged 15 rebounds per game. Nater had been with the club since 1977.

In the early 1980s, the Clippers underwent more changes. Before the 1980–81 season, the team fired Shue and hired Paul Silas as coach. Silas had only recently retired as a player after 16 seasons in the NBA. The Clippers also traded Free to the Golden State Warriors in exchange for a first-round draft pick and guard Phil Smith.

San Diego's Swen Nater, *left*, battles Golden State's Clifford Ray in November 1980. The Clippers slumped in the early 1980s, but Nater was an elite rebounder.

The Clippers were headed for one of their most dismal periods. They went 36–46 in 1980–81 and fell all the way to a 17–65 in 1981–82. The 17–65 record was the worst in the club's existence. Already without Walton, the Clippers also did not have Nater for much of that season because of a knee injury. On top of that, the team traded Smith and Freeman Williams during the season. The guards had been productive players for San Diego.

The 1981–82 campaign was the first of three straight in which the Clippers finished in last place in the Pacific Division. Off the court, the biggest change was in ownership. Donald T. Sterling bought the

Clippers forward Terry Cummings goes up for a shot versus the Sonics in December 1982. Cummings was the NBA Rookie of the Year for the 1982–83 season.

Clippers from Irv Levin on June 16, 1981. Sterling was a lawyer and real estate mogul. He lived in Beverly Hills, an affluent suburb of Los Angeles. The change in owners would eventually lead to the end of the NBA in San Diego.

The Clippers' attendance dropped off during the 1981–82 season. Sterling indicated he might move the team to Los Angeles. The San Diego Sports Arena seated about 13,000. That capacity is considered small by today's NBA arena standards. But it was not necessarily so small at the time. Still, the Clippers' poor play led to shrinking crowds.

San Diego went 25–57 in the 1982–83 season and 30–52

in 1983–84. There were some individual highlights, however. Walton played in 33 and 55 games those seasons for his hometown team. Also, two future All-Stars began their NBA careers with the Clippers during this time. Forward Tom Chambers was the team's leading scorer as a rookie in 1981–82. He averaged 17.2 points per game.

The next season, forward Terry Cummings averaged 23.7 points and 10.6 rebounds and was named NBA Rookie of the Year. Despite some signs of progress, Sterling had made his mind up about relocating the Clippers. He moved the team up the California coast to Los Angeles before the 1984–85 season. The Clippers would play their home games at the Los Angeles Sports Arena.

The Clippers' six-season record in San Diego was 186–306. They had just one winning season and made no playoff appearances during that span. Unfortunately for the Clippers, a change in location from San Diego to Los Angeles would not result in a change in the team's fortunes.

LEAVING FOR LOS ANGELES

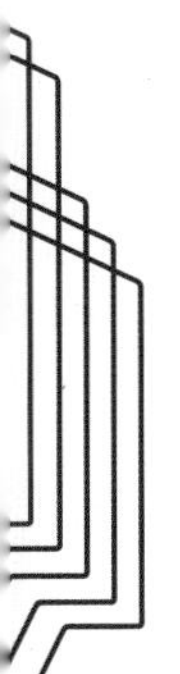

The Clippers moved to Los Angeles in time for the 1984–85 season. Although they had a new home, they were the same old struggling Clippers.

The Clippers suffered a losing record in each of their first seven seasons in Los Angeles. The Lakers overshadowed the Clippers during this time. The Lakers won NBA titles in 1985, 1987, and 1988. The Lakers had remarkable players such as Magic Johnson and Kareem Abdul-Jabbar. The team played in front of big crowds at the Forum in Inglewood. Hollywood stars such as Jack Nicholson sat in the courtside seats.

The Clippers, meanwhile, had aging veterans and journeymen. The Clippers' home venue, the Los Angeles Sports

Bill Walton releases a shot in an October 1984 exhibition game before the Clippers' first season in Los Angeles. The team's struggles continued in its new city.

Arena, did not provide much glamour.

The Clippers tried their best to gain attention. Before its first season in Los Angeles, the team traded forward Terry Cummings to the Milwaukee Bucks. The Clippers received forwards Marques Johnson and Junior Bridgeman, center Harvey Catchings, and cash. The Clippers gave up Cummings and guards Ricky Pierce and Craig Hodges. The team also drafted forward Michael Cage in 1984. Cage had starred at San Diego State University. He would become one of the NBA's top rebounders.

In the 1984–85 season, center Bill Walton was healthier. He played in 67 games for the Clippers and averaged 10.1 points and nine rebounds. Still, the team finished 31–51.

After that season, the Clippers traded Walton to the Celtics for forward Cedric Maxwell, cash, and a first-round draft pick. Walton helped Boston win an NBA title in 1986. He also captured the league's Sixth Man Award. That is just how it went with the Clippers.

The Clippers' second season in Los Angeles was not much better. This was the case

The Clippers' Michael Cage secures the ball during the 1987–88 season, when he led the NBA with an average of more than 13 rebounds per game.

even with first-round draft pick Benoit Benjamin, a 7-foot center, added to the mix. The Clippers finished 32–50. Owner Donald Sterling then decided to hire Elgin Baylor as general manager. Baylor was a star forward for the Lakers from 1958 to 1971.

In Baylor's first season in charge, the Clippers finished a club-worst 12–70. Don Chaney, the coach since the 1984–85 season, was fired. Gene Shue rejoined the team as coach. But things barely got better in 1987–88, when the Clippers finished 17–65.

The Clippers' Danny Manning, *right*, and Ron Harper talk during the 1989–90 season. A knee injury sidelined Harper for most of that campaign, when the Clippers went 30–52.

It seemed that the Clippers finally found some good luck in May 1988. That month, they won the lottery for the NBA Draft. This gave them the league's top draft pick the next month. The club used it to select 6-foot-10 forward Danny Manning. Manning had led the University of Kansas to the NCAA title that year. Clippers fans were excited. Season-ticket sales doubled.

But good fortune did not follow the Clippers. Manning suffered a knee injury and missed the last 56 games of his rookie season. Shue did not finish the season either. Don Casey, a former Chicago Bulls assistant, replaced him. The Clippers limped to a 21–61 record.

The Clippers' continual losing began to affect them in unusual ways. The team had the second pick in the 1989 NBA Draft. Los Angeles chose forward Danny Ferry of Duke University. But he refused to sign with the Clippers. Instead, he took a $1 million offer from a team in Italy. Shortly into the 1989–90 season, Baylor traded Ferry's rights and forward Reggie Williams to the Cleveland Cavaliers for guard Ron Harper and three draft choices.

Manning returned for the 1989–90 season. He averaged 16.3 points and 5.9 rebounds. But Harper suffered a major knee injury, just as Manning had the season before. The Clippers finished with another losing record at 30–52.

DANNY MANNING

Forward Danny Manning was the face of the franchise from the time the Clippers drafted him first overall in 1988 until they traded him to the Atlanta Hawks on February 24, 1994.

Manning had achieved much success by the time he reached the NBA. He helped the University of Kansas reach the NCAA Final Four in 1986 and again in 1988, when the Jayhawks won the national title. Manning also played for the United States team that won the bronze medal in the 1988 Summer Olympics.

Manning was a capable scorer and a strong passer. His father, Ed, also played in the league. Danny Manning made two NBA All-Star Game appearances while he was a Clipper. Unfortunately, knee injuries hampered him. His last season was in 2002–03 with the Detroit Pistons. He averaged 14 points and 5.2 rebounds in his NBA career.

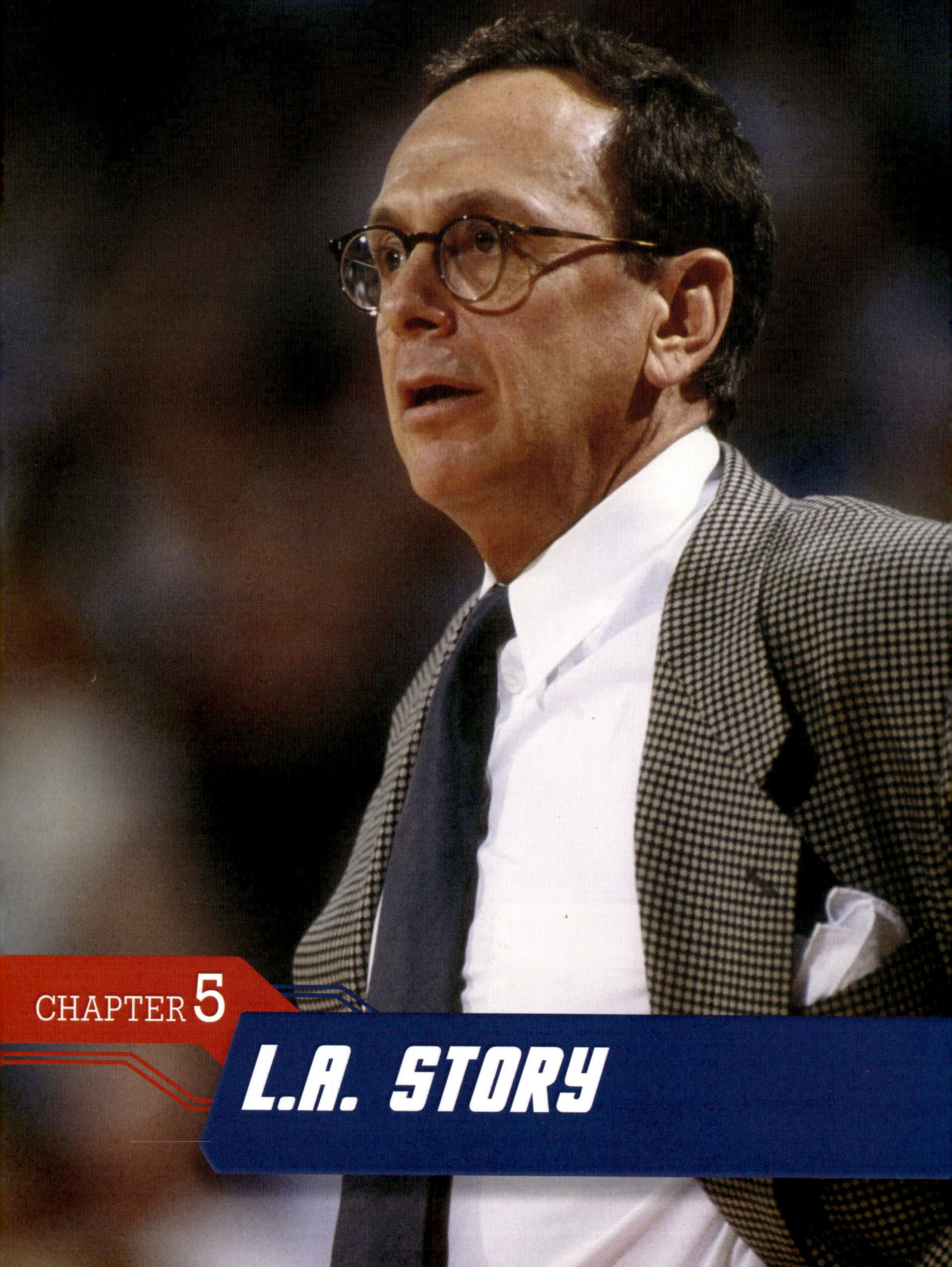

CHAPTER 5

L.A. STORY

All the moves Clippers general manager Elgin Baylor had been making finally started to pay off in the early 1990s.

Danny Manning and Ron Harper were healthy and playing well. The Clippers added veteran point guard Doc Rivers. After 16 years, the franchise returned to the playoffs in 1991–92. But it took some doing.

The Clippers had three coaches that season but still finished 45–37. After the team started 21–24, coach Mike Schuler was fired. Assistant coach Mack Calvin replaced him for two games. Baylor then hired Larry Brown, who had coached several NBA and college teams. Brown coached Manning at the University of Kansas. Brown inspired the Clippers. They won 23 of their final 35 games.

Finally, there was excitement surrounding the Clippers.

Larry Brown, shown in November 1992, coached the Clippers to the playoffs in 1992 and 1993. The postseason berths were the club's first since 1976.

As the number seven seed in the 1992 postseason, the Clippers drew the second-seeded Utah Jazz in the first round. The host Jazz easily won the first two games. The Clippers took Game 3 at home and stayed alive in the best-of-five series.

Game 4 was scheduled to be held the Sports Arena. But deadly rioting broke out in Los Angeles after four white police officers accused of beating an African-American motorist were acquitted. They were cleared of the charges even though a bystander had captured the beating incident on video. The riots forced authorities to postpone all sporting events in Los Angeles.

It would not be possible, then, to play Game 4 at the Sports Arena. So the game was moved about 35 miles (56 km) south to the Anaheim Convention Center. Los Angeles won 115–107. Manning had 33 points and 10 rebounds. The series went back to Utah for Game 5. The Jazz rallied for a 98–89 win.

Before the 1992–93 campaign, the Clippers received point guard Mark Jackson from New York and center Stanley Roberts from Orlando in trades. The Clippers finished 41–41 and made the postseason again. Los Angeles, the seventh seed,

Clippers general manager Elgin Baylor announces the departure of coach Larry Brown in May 1993. The Clippers would not be as successful without Brown.

would face the second-seeded Houston Rockets in the first round. Los Angeles won two of the first four games. Houston won Game 5 84–80 to take the series.

More changes were coming for the Clippers. Brown left to coach the Indiana Pacers before the 1993–94 season. Veteran NBA coach Bob Weiss replaced him. Then, in February 1994, the Clippers traded Manning to the Atlanta Hawks for forward Dominique Wilkins. But Wilkins's best days were behind him. After two playoff seasons, the Clippers finished 27–55.

It only got worse. Weiss was fired. Longtime NBA coach Bill Fitch replaced him. The Clippers finished 17–65 in 1994–95. In 1995–96, the Clippers improved to 29–53.

From left, Quentin Richardson, Darius Miles, Lamar Odom, and Corey Maggette pose in October 2000. The Clippers had young talent during that era but did not win many games.

The team returned to the playoffs in 1996–97, even with a 36–46 record. But the Jazz swept the Clippers in three games.

Then another playoff drought followed. The Clippers would miss the postseason for the next eight seasons. They won only 17 games in 1997–98, leading to Fitch's firing. After that season, the Clippers won the lottery for the top pick in the 1998 NBA Draft. The club used it to select center Michael Olowokandi of the University of the Pacific in California. During Olowokandi's time with the Clippers, he was mediocre at best.

The 1998–99 NBA season was shortened because the

owners and the players could not reach a labor agreement. Play finally began in February 1999. The Clippers finished an ugly 9–41.

The Clippers moved into a new home arena, the Staples Center. But they had gone back to their old ways. They finished 15–67 and 31–51 the next two seasons. Baylor kept trying, though. During the 2001 NBA Draft, he made a deal with the Chicago Bulls. He brought forward Elton Brand to Los Angeles in exchange for forward Brian Skinner and center Tyson Chandler's draft rights.

Brand's rebounding and scoring helped the Clippers go 39–43 in 2001–02. However, Los Angeles would not reach that victory total in any of the next three seasons. This was the case even though the Clippers had talented young players such as guard Quentin Richardson, forwards Corey Maggette and Lamar Odom, and center Chris Kaman.

The Clippers hired veteran NBA coach Mike Dunleavy before the 2003–04 season. Los Angeles improved by nine victories and went 37–45 in 2004–05. The club then acquired guard Sam Cassell before the 2005–06 season. That move helped the Clippers go 47–35 and make the playoffs. The Clippers reached the second round, matching a club record. But they fell to the Phoenix Suns in seven games.

True to team history, the Clippers could not maintain their success. The club finished 40–42 in 2006–07 and fell short of the playoffs. Brand continued his strong play. But Cassell had lost a step. The Clippers dropped to 23–59 in 2007–08.

Brand left the Clippers, signing with the Philadelphia 76ers before the 2008–09 season. The Clippers went 19–63 that season.

The Clippers won the lottery for the 2009 NBA Draft. With the top choice, they selected former University of Oklahoma star forward Blake Griffin. But bad luck followed the Clippers again. Griffin injured his left knee in the preseason and missed the entire 2009–10 campaign. Los Angeles finished 29–53. Dunleavy stepped aside as coach during the season to focus on his duties as general manager.

Things were starting to look more promising for the Clippers in 2010–11. The team had hired former Chicago Bulls coach Vinny Del Negro before the season. Also, Griffin returned and excelled. The 6-foot-10 Griffin set a team record with 27 consecutive double-doubles. He reached double figures in both

The Clippers' Blake Griffin emerged as one of the NBA's top young stars in the 2010–11 season. Griffin's leaping ability helped him to win the 2011 All-Star Slam Dunk Contest.

points and rebounds in those games. Griffin also thrilled fans with his acrobatic dunks.

Despite Griffin's emergence and guard Eric Gordon's further development as a scorer, the Clippers were still a losing team. But they appeared to have two young stars who could lead the franchise. Fans were hopeful that the team's next playoff berth, and perhaps even a first league title, could happen soon.

1970
On October 14, the Buffalo Braves win the first regular-season game in franchise history, defeating the visiting Cleveland Cavaliers 107–92.

1972
On April 10, the Braves select center/forward Bob McAdoo with the second overall pick in the NBA Draft. McAdoo had starred at the University of North Carolina.

1974
McAdoo averages an NBA-best 30.6 points per game, and the Braves finish the season with a 42–40 record and qualify for their first postseason berth.

1975
For a second straight season, McAdoo leads the NBA in scoring. He averages a career-high 34.5 points a contest and is named league MVP.

1978
On April 9, the team plays its last game as the Buffalo Braves, a 131–114 road loss to the Celtics.

1979
San Diego native Bill Walton, who had been a star center with the Portland Trail Blazers, signs with his hometown Clippers on May 13.

1981
Beverly Hills, California, attorney and real estate developer Donald Sterling buys the Clippers on June 16.

1984
On April 14, the franchise plays its final game as the San Diego Clippers, beating the visiting Utah Jazz 146–128.

1988
On June 28, the Clippers select former University of Kansas star forward Danny Manning with the top overall pick in the NBA Draft.

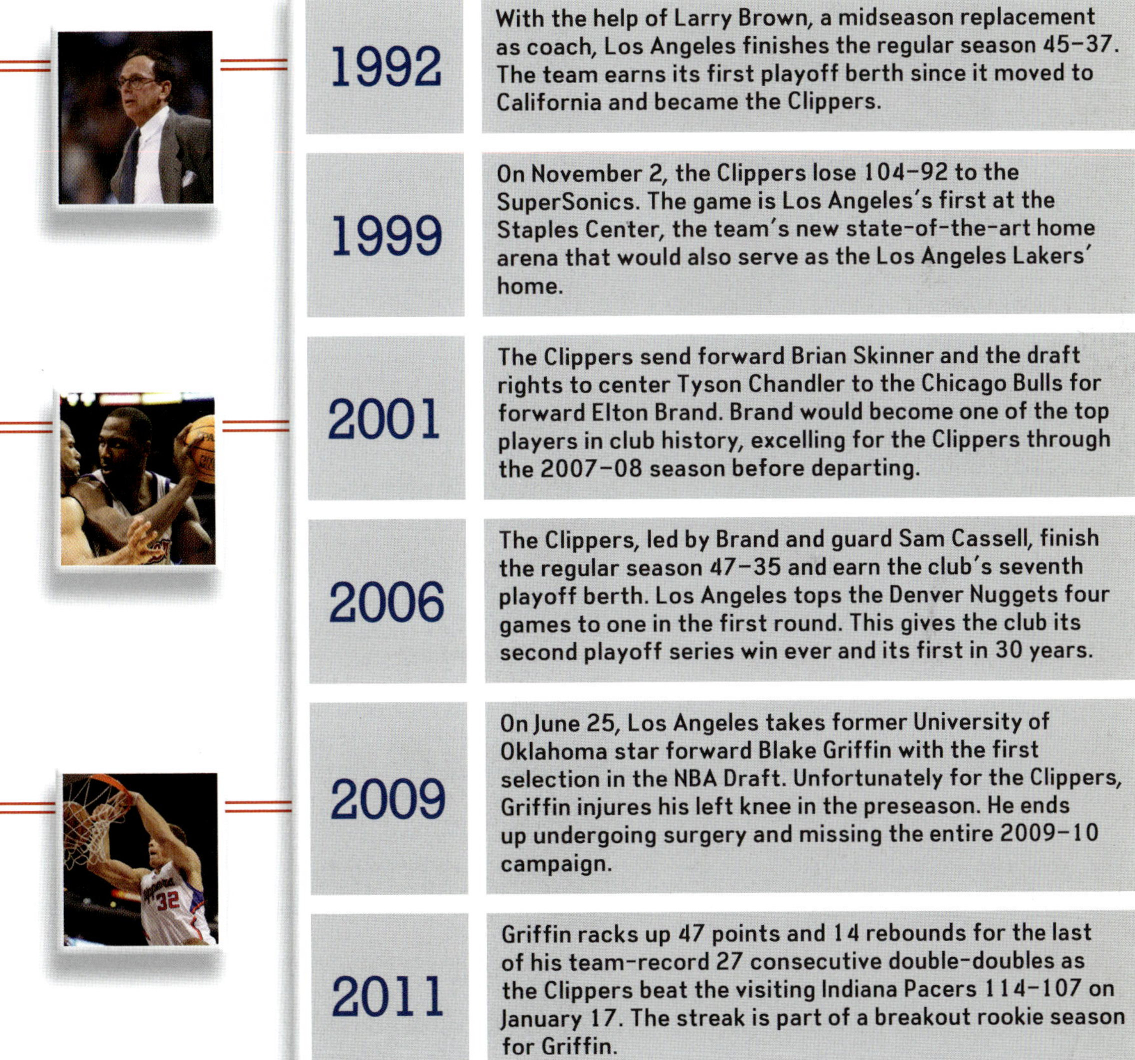

1992	With the help of Larry Brown, a midseason replacement as coach, Los Angeles finishes the regular season 45–37. The team earns its first playoff berth since it moved to California and became the Clippers.
1999	On November 2, the Clippers lose 104–92 to the SuperSonics. The game is Los Angeles's first at the Staples Center, the team's new state-of-the-art home arena that would also serve as the Los Angeles Lakers' home.
2001	The Clippers send forward Brian Skinner and the draft rights to center Tyson Chandler to the Chicago Bulls for forward Elton Brand. Brand would become one of the top players in club history, excelling for the Clippers through the 2007–08 season before departing.
2006	The Clippers, led by Brand and guard Sam Cassell, finish the regular season 47–35 and earn the club's seventh playoff berth. Los Angeles tops the Denver Nuggets four games to one in the first round. This gives the club its second playoff series win ever and its first in 30 years.
2009	On June 25, Los Angeles takes former University of Oklahoma star forward Blake Griffin with the first selection in the NBA Draft. Unfortunately for the Clippers, Griffin injures his left knee in the preseason. He ends up undergoing surgery and missing the entire 2009–10 campaign.
2011	Griffin racks up 47 points and 14 rebounds for the last of his team-record 27 consecutive double-doubles as the Clippers beat the visiting Indiana Pacers 114–107 on January 17. The streak is part of a breakout rookie season for Griffin.

FRANCHISE HISTORY

Buffalo Braves (1970–78)
San Diego Clippers (1978–84)
Los Angeles Clippers (1984–)

NBA FINALS

None

PLAYOFF APPEARANCES

1974, 1975, 1976, 1992, 1993, 1997, 2006

KEY PLAYERS
(position[s]; years with team)

Elton Brand (F; 2001–08)
Sam Cassell (G; 2005–08)
Terry Cummings (F; 1982–84)
Ernie DiGregorio (G; 1973–77)
World B. Free (G; 1978–80)
Eric Gordon (G; 2008–)
Blake Griffin (F; 2010–)
Ron Harper (G/F; 1989–94)
Chris Kaman (C; 2003–)
Danny Manning (F/C; 1988–94)
Bob McAdoo (C/F; 1972–77)
Swen Nater (C; 1977–83)
Lamar Odom (F; 1999–2003)
Charles Smith (F/C; 1988–92)
Elmore Smith (C; 1971–73)
Randy Smith (G; 1971–79, 1982–83)
Bill Walton (C/F; 1979–80, 1982–85)

KEY COACHES

Larry Brown (1992–93):
    64–53; 4–6 (postseason)
Mike Dunleavy (2003–10):
    215–326; 7–5 (postseason)
Jack Ramsay (1972–76):
    158–170; 9–13 (postseason)

HOME ARENAS

Buffalo Memorial Auditorium
    (1970–78)
San Diego Sports Arena (1978–84)
Los Angeles Sports Arena (1984–99)
Staples Center (1999–)

* All statistics through 2010–11 season

"This hurts, but we shocked the world, 100 percent of the world, everybody but us." —Clippers guard Sam Cassell, after the team advanced to the second round of the 2006 playoffs before falling to the Phoenix Suns

San Diego's basketball history is not limited to the two NBA franchises, the Rockets and the Clippers, that the city lost. San Diego also was home to a club in the ABA, which was a rival league to the NBA and existed from 1967 to 1976. The San Diego team was called the Conquistadors and began play in 1972. Before the 1975–76 ABA campaign, the team changed its name to the Sails. The franchise folded after just 11 games that season, however. The ABA itself went out of business after that season. The Conquistadors/Sails did not have a winning record in any of their seasons.

"For so long we were the other team in the city. When the Lakers would come in here, it was like a home game for them in their road uniforms." —Clippers forward Danny Manning, on what it was like to be overshadowed by the Lakers in Los Angeles

On November 5, 1993, Clippers rookie guard Terry Dehere made his NBA debut in Los Angeles's 97–95 home win over the Portland Trail Blazers. The next day, a racehorse named Dehere ran in the $1 million Breeders' Cup Juvenile race at Santa Anita Park in the Los Angeles suburb of Arcadia. The horse finished out of the money. Dehere the racehorse was named after Dehere the basketball player, who had played at Seton Hall University in New Jersey before joining the Clippers. Seton Hall alumnus Robert Brennan named several of his racehorses after former Seton Hall Pirates players such as Dehere.

GLOSSARY

assist

A pass that leads directly to a made basket.

attendance

The number of fans at a particular game or who come to watch a team play during a particular season.

contract

A binding agreement about, for example, years of commitment by a basketball player in exchange for a given salary.

double-double

When a player reaches double digits in two different categories during one game, such as points, assists, rebounds, steals, or blocked shots.

draft

A system used by professional sports leagues to select new players in order to spread incoming talent among all teams. The NBA Draft is held each June.

expansion

In sports, the addition of a franchise or franchises to a league.

free agent

A player whose contract has expired and who is able to sign with a team of his choice.

general manager

The executive who is in charge of the team's overall operation. He or she hires and fires coaches, drafts players, and signs free agents.

rebound

To secure the basketball after a missed shot.

rookie

A first-year player in the NBA.

sixth man

The best substitute on a basketball team. He or she typically is the first player to come off the bench to replace a starter.

Further Reading

Ballard, Chris. *The Art of a Beautiful Game: The Thinking Fan's Tour of the NBA*. New York: Simon & Schuster, 2009.

Simmons, Bill. *The Book of Basketball: The NBA According to the Sports Guy*. New York: Random House, 2009.

Wendel, Tim. *Buffalo, Home of the Braves*. Traverse City, MI: SunBear Press, 2009.

Web Links

To learn more about the Los Angeles Clippers, visit ABDO Publishing Company online at **www.abdopublishing.com.** Web sites about the Clippers are featured on our Book Links page. These links are routinely monitored and updated to provide the most current information available.

Places to Visit

Naismith Memorial Basketball Hall of Fame
1000 West Columbus Avenue
Springfield, MA 01105
413-781-6500
www.hoophall.com
This hall of fame and museum highlights the greatest players and moments in the history of basketball. Bob McAdoo and Bill Walton are among the former Clippers who are enshrined here.

Staples Center
1111 South Figueroa Street
Los Angeles, CA 90015
213-742-7326
www.staplescenter.com
This has been the Clippers' home arena since the 1999–2000 season. They play 41 regular-season games here each season.

Valley View Casino Center
3500 Sports Arena Boulevard
San Diego, CA 92110
619-224-4171
valleyviewcasinocenter.com
This arena, formerly known as the San Diego Sports Arena, was home to the Clippers when they played in San Diego. These days, it plays host to various entertainment and sports events.

INDEX

About the Author

Bernie Wilson has worked for The Associated Press since 1984, based in Spokane, Washington; Los Angeles, California; and San Diego, California. He covered the Clippers and the Lakers of the NBA and the Kings of the NHL while he was based in Los Angeles from 1987 to 1991. Based in San Diego since 1991, he covers the Padres, the Chargers, and San Diego State University. He also covers the America's Cup and has reported from seven Olympics.